ADVENTURE TIME

SUGARY SHORTS

kaboom!™

CN
CARTOON NETWORK.   FREDERATOR

ROSS RICHIE CEO & Founder • JACK CUMMINS President & COO • MARK SMYLIE Chief Creative Officer • MATT GAGNON Editor-in-Chief • FILIP SABLIK VP of Publishing & Marketing • STEPHEN CHRISTY VP of Development
LANCE KREITER VP of Licensing & Merchandising • PHIL BARBARO VP of Finance • BRYCE CARLSON Managing Editor • MEL CAYLO Marketing Manager • SCOTT NEWMAN Production Design Manager • IRENE BRADISH Operations Manager • DAFNA PLEBAN Editor
SHANNON WATTERS Editor • ERIC HARBURN Editor • REBECCA TAYLOR Editor • CHRIS ROSA Assistant Editor • ALEX GALER Assistant Editor • WHITNEY LEOPARD Assistant Editor • JASMINE AMIRI Assistant Editor • CAMERON CHITTOCK Assistant Editor
HANNAH NANCE PARTLOW Production Designer • DEVIN FUNCHES E-Commerce & Inventory Coordinator • BRIANNA HART Executive Assistant • AARON FERRARA Operations Assistant • JOSÉ MEZA Sales Assistant • ELIZABETH LOUGHRIDGE Accounting Assistant

ADVENTURE TIME

CREATED BY
PENDLETON WARD

Cover by
LOGAN FAERBER

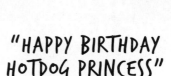

"LUMPY SPACE DRAMA"
Written and Illustrated by
ZAC GORMAN

"FISHLING"
Written and Illustrated by
**SHANE &
CHRIS HOUGHTON**
Colors by Josh Uhlich

"THE MEANING OF BRAVERY"
Written and Illustrated by
ZACK GIALLONGO
Colors by Lisa Moore

"THE DEVILISH
DEVOURER OF DELICIOUS
DELICACIES"
Written and Illustrated by
JOSH LESNICK

"HAPPY BIRTHDAY
HOTDOG PRINCESS"
Written and Illustrated by
**FRANK GIBSON &
BECKY DREISTADT**

"HOT DEALS IN
ICE KINGDOM"
Written by
JON M. GIBSON
Illustrated by
JIM RUGG

"THE ICE KING AND HIS
MAGICAL MATCHMAKING
MINI-COMIC"
Written by
ALEXIS FREDERICK-FROST
Illustrated by
ANDREW ARNOLD

"PRINCESS OF RAD HATS"
Written and Illustrated by
CHRIS SCHWEIZER

Assistant Editor
WHITNEY LEOPARD

Editor
SHANNON WATTERS

Designer
HANNAH NANCE PARTLOW

With Special Thanks to Marisa Marionakis, Rick Blanco, Curtis Lelash, Laurie Halal-Ono,
Keith Mack, Kelly Crews and the wonderful folks at Cartoon Network.

MY CIDER
THE MOUNTAIN

My Cider the Mountain

Why, hello Princess Bubblegum! I got the cider I made for Cinnamon Bun's birthday party right here!

Huh? OH!

I thought I *canceled* that order, Tree Trunks!

I pressed it from the ELUSIVE Subrosa Sweet! My FAVORITE APPLE!

Are you EVEN LISTENING, Tree Trunks? I CANCELED THAT ORDER!

WHAT?! WHY? I thought you and Cinnamon Bun LIKED it!

HAHA! I did, but I LOVE the MYSTERIOUS CIDER from the SKY!

Cider from the...

Here comes a batch NOW!

Aw CRUMBS!

No matter... Someone get Cinnamon Bun to mop up this MESS! CHOP!CHOP!

CLAP! CLAP! CLAP!

WELL, where is he?! I can't mop it up! I need to... um... choose the NAPKINS! The party is TONIGHT!

The cider is very good... but it tastes ...FAMILIAR.

Farewell y'all! Princess Bubblegum, I'll miss you!

Okay! Sure! See you!

At least the forest critters still like my cider...

SNAP!

WHAT WAS THAT?!

SNAP!

CRUNCH!

!

Who could *THAT* be? I'm the only one livin' on this here mountain.

It looked like a ... like a MUMMY!

Where is it going?

It's going right near the orchard ...

...where the Subrosa Sweet apple grows!

Maybe this was a bad ide-OH!

Cider! I was RIGHT! That creature IS the other cider maker!

That FLAVOR! It uses the Subrosa Sweet! I'm sure of it! But it's also got a ... MUSKY... almost CINNAMON aftertaste...

Every morning I get up, drink three gallons of your cider... my FAVORITE.

Aw, SHUCKS, Cinnamon Bun!

Then I wrap myself in rags and go for a jog!

Then I drink more and jog again!

Then I come HERE!

♪ Just RELAXIN' and SWEATIN' out my IMPURITIES! ♪

Well...if it's not YOU...

...Who's leaving the cider out your window?

H'yuk! That's not CIDER!

That's where I SQUEEZE my dirty towels and SWEAT RAGS.

And the song birds just... take it away!

Well... I better go! I don't wanna be late for my own party!

HAPPY BIRTHDAY CINNAMON BUN!

JAKE... this stuff tastes like a DONUT'S ARMPIT!

AND HOW would YOU know what a donut's arm pit TASTES like, DUDE?

Uhh... Umm...

HEE HEE! IT DOES! It tastes EXACTLY like my ARMPIT!

renier

LAUNDROMARCELINE

ISSUE TWO, COVER D
FRANK AND BECKY

What's up?

Oof

DUMP

There was a red-splosion in my laundry. I was hoping you could help fix it!

WHAT

You want me...

A vampire queen...

...to do...

...Your LAUNDRY?

Wait! Wait! Marceline!

I can help you in exchange! Do chores, whatever!

Oh.

Actually there **are** a few things you could do around here...

AFTER THE SHOW

—ZAC GORMAN

END

BACON FIELDS

ISSUE THREE, COVER D
STEPHANIE BUSCEMA

BACON FIELDS BY MICHAEL DEFORGE

THE RIDE OF SIR SLICER

ISSUE FOUR, COVER B.
KASSANDRA HELLER

The Ride of Sir Slicer

—ZAC GORMAN

THE ULTIMATE
PARTY DIP

EMIT ERUTNEVDA

ISSUE FIVE, COVER B
ELEANOR DAVIS

I DON'T REALLY KNOW!

...BUT IT'S LOUD AND THERE SURE ARE A LOT OF LINES!

AVE YOU ED LOOKING OUGH THE THER SIDE?

DIDN'T OCCUR TO ME A HOLE HAS ANOTHER SIDE.

HERE, YOU HOLD IT...

WOAH!

WHAT? WHAT?!

FOLD.

I FOLD TOO.

FOLD

CALL-

AGAIN?

...I'M STARTING TO THINK YOU'RE EITHER THE WORLD'S GREATEST POKER ACE, OR ELSE YOU'RE A TOTAL CARD CHEAT!!

NEITHER!

...I'M MAGIC, DUDES.

FIN...

ICE KINGDUMB

ISSUE FIVE, COVER D
MIKE "GABE" KRAHULIK

ICE KING DUMB

Oh, Gunter, I am TIRED of being rejected by ONE princess after ANOTHER.

wak

Gunter's RIGHT. I AM a king. What I REALLY need isn't a princess at ALL.

I need a QUEEN.

FLAP
FLAP
FLAP
FLAP

FLAP
FLAP

What do YOU want?

You're going to MARRY me, Vampire Queen. Or ELSE.

FLAP

Oh, YEAH?

LANDW

RARGH

KLINK
KLINK

I'll stick with PRINCESSES.

Queens are SCARY.

FLAP FLAP FLAP

ZOOM

FLAP FLAP

Guys can be so dumb...

END

LEVEL 99

LEVEL 99

by ANTHONY CLARK

FINN!

FINN!

FINN!

FINNNNNNNNNNNNNNNN!

WHAT, MAN? WHAT'S GOING ON?

COME DOWNSTAIRS! BMO AND I HAVE A SURPRISE FOR YOU!

A SURPRISE? I LOVE THOSE!

LOOK, YOU CAN'T JUST—

HEY, WHAT ARE YOU GUYS DOING?

CAN I BE IN YOUR MOVIE?

NO.

BUT I'M REALLY GOOD AT ACTING. WATCH THIS!

I'M SKATEBOARDING. PRETTY COOL, HUH?

WE CAN CALL IT "SKATEBOARD: THE MOVIE."

IT PROBABLY COULD HAVE USED SOME MORE EDITING, BUT I... I HAD A LOT OF STUFF TO DO.

SNRKKKK

HEH.

THANKS, YOU GUYS.

JUST KNOWING YOU BELIEVE IN ME HAS GOTTEN ME SUPER PUMPED.

BMO, LET'S DO THIS.

yayyy

WIZARD WARS

/ NEW GAME

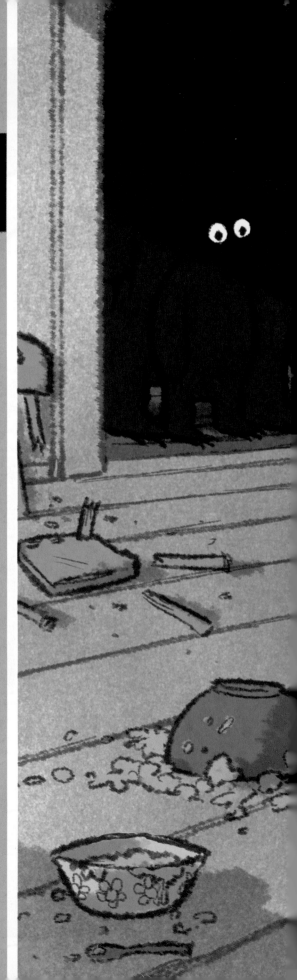

TIME WAITS
FOR NO ONE

ISSUE SEVEN, COVER C
GRAHAM ANNABEL

TIME WAITS FOR NO ONE
WRITTEN AND DRAWN BY SHANNON WHEELER

I WANT TO MAKE A *TIME* MACHINE.

I DO TOO, BUT WE HAVE TO BE *CAREFUL*.

WHY?

NOT A LOT IS KNOWN ABOUT *TIME TRAVEL.*

ONE *THEORY* SAYS THAT TIME IS AN *ILLUSION.*

PAST, PRESENT AND FUTURE EXIST *SIMULTANEOUSLY.*

TIME IS A ROAD WE *THINK* WE'RE WALKING DOWN. IF WE WERE MORE *EVOLVED* WE'D *STEP OFF* THE ROAD AND SEE *EVERYTHING* AT ONCE.

WOW.

APOLOGIES TO KURT VONNEGUT

POLOGIES TO RAY BRADBURY

THERE COULD BE *MULTIPLE TIMELINES.*

LIKE AN *INFINITE TREE* WITH *INFINITE BRANCHES.* EVERY CHOICE WE'VE EVER MADE CREATES A *NEW REALITY.*

WORLDS WITH *CANDY ZOMBIES* OR JAKE AND FINN *NEVER MEET* AND TIME LINES WHERE *WE DON'T EVEN EXIST.*

GO BACK IN TIME AND YOU'LL BE TANGLED IN ANY NUMBER OF *ALTERNATE REALITIES.*

SCARY.

FINDING YOUR WAY HOME TO THE RIGHT TIMELINE COULD BE *IMPOSSIBLE.*

APOLOGIES TO LARRY NIVEN

TIME TRAVEL COULD DESTROY ALL REALITY BY CREATING A LOOP.

LOOP?

IT'S A LOOP. IF YOU USE A TIME MACHINE YOU GO BACK IN TIME AND EVERYTHING SEEMS GREAT.

GREAT!

UNTIL THE MOMENT YOU INVENT THE TIME MACHINE AND YOU GO BACK IN TIME... AGAIN.

EVERYONE IS TRAPPED FOREVER IN A LOOP... DOING THE SAME THING OVER AND OVER.

LOOP?

THE FUTURE WOULD CEASE TO EXIST.

LOOP?

I WANT TO MAKE A TIME MACHINE.

I DO TOO BUT WE HAVE TO BE CAREFUL.

.POLOGIES TO MICHAEL T. GILBERT

END

LUMPY SPACE DRAMA

-ZAC GORMAN

HAPPY BIRTHDAY HOT DOG PRINCESS

ISSUE EIGHT, COVER D

PHIL McANDREW

As a gesture of friendship from the Candy Kingdom, I agree to grant you one birthday wish... if it isn't completely difficult or awful

Well... When I was very young, I lost my beloved bun.

If only we could be re-united one last time...

BooRooo

Oh, that guy.

Peppermint Butler! I command you to re-unite Hot Dog Princess with her beloved bun!

Fine. It shall be done.

We must stare where two walls meet to begin our journey!

Is that all?!

Where have you taken me?

Today we walk in the Land of the Dead. Horrors beyond comprehension await us on our quest to Death's domain.

A princess fears nothing! I will make this "Death" return my prince to me!

Your *PRINCE?!*

That wasn't too bad! Where is this Death fellow?

You do not understand that which you are about to face.

Why, hello Butler! Who is your friend?

HAHA HA HAHA HA HA HA HA

I am not his friend, I am a princess and I am here to retrieve my beloved bun from your vile clutches!

Really? That guy? He's out back, but first Butler must pay the price!

What have
I done!

I'm fine. We
should go.

Have fun
with the bun!

HAW
HAW
HAW
HAW

MY BELOVED BUN!

Hey, man. Want to play some tetherball?

I am whole once more!

Whoa. Chill out, man.

But I came to rescue you!

No way, man. I have everything I could ever want here. Soda. Tetherball. A vast wasteland.

FISHLING

ISSUE NINE, COVER D
JON VERMILYEA

"FISHSLING"

WHAT KINDA BAIT ARE YOU GONNA USE, JAKE?

I'M JUST GONNA REACH AROUND DOWN THERE AND PULL OUT THE BIGGEST FISH!

HAHA! YEAH RIGHT! I'LL BET I CAN CATCH A BIGGER FISH THAN YOU, DUDE.

YOU'RE ON!

SUPER INTENSE FISHING!

...

WRITTEN BY: SHANE HOUGHTON   DRAWN BY: CHRIS HOUGHTON   COLORED BY: JOSH ULRICH

*JOSÉ, FOR ALL YOU NON-SPANISH SPEAKERS.

SOON...

I CAUGHT THE BIGGEST FISH IN THE POND! THAT FAT BABY IS MINE!

I CAN'T BELIEVE ALL THOSE FISH JUST KEPT EATING EACH OTHER.

FISH ARE WEIRD.

I WIN, DUDE.

AH, POOP!

ROOOAAARR!!!

I'M LIKE, SO AFRAID OF FISH!

THAT'S **YOUR** FISH ON ITS WAY TO DESTROY CANDY KINGDOM, BRO.

NO WAY, FATHER IN SPANISH!*

* PADRE, FOR ALL YOU NON-SPANISH SPEAKERS.

I GUESS WE BETTER GO KILL IT.

mmhmm.

FISH FINISHING FINALE!

DUDE.

ON THE ACCOUNT OF BEING EATEN AND EVERYTHING, I THINK WE SHOULD CALL THE CONTEST A DRAW.

TOTES. WE'RE BOTH PRETTY DOPE FISHER-FOLKS.

LET'S GET OUT OF HERE. I LIKE EATING FISH BETTER THAN BEING EATEN BY FISH.

I'LL BE THE LINE, YOU BE THE BAIT.

I'LL TAKE OFF MY SHOES 'CAUSE FISH LOVE TOESIES.

?!

WAHOO!

SHOULDN'T I HAVE SUFFOCATED BY NOW?

HOT DEALS IN
ICE KINGDOM

ISSUE TEN, COVER B
TYSON HESSE

THE MEANING
OF BRAVERY

THE MEANING OF BRAVERY
BY ZACK GIALLONGO

SUSAN IS HERE TO WRECK MONSTERS.

THAT SO?

WHA-? BEAT UP? MONSTER?

NO, NO! *THEY'RE* THE MONSTERS!

DRAT, THERE THEY GO...

DEFEAT MONSTERS, BECOME BRAVE.

THUMP!

I SEE! I CAN HELP YOU FIND MORE EVIL THINGS UNDERGROUND TO DEFEAT, THEN!

Twitch

Twitch

YOU?

OF COURSE! I'D LOVE TO HELP YOU BECOME BRAVE!

WE'LL MAKE A GREAT TEAM. NOW, OFF YOU GO! DOWN THIS TUNNEL.

GOOD DAY!

EH?

WHAT ARE YOU DOING HERE?

KICKING YOU OUT.

EARN SOME BRAVERY, SUSAN!

BUT...

DO IT!

WOMP!

WELCOME, WANDERERS.

THAT GIANT MORON IS A THORN IN MY PAW AND YOUR TICKET TO BRAVERY!

SUSAN WILL BE BRAVE. FIGHT ME!

I CANNOT, YOUNG WARRIOR.

BUT, SUSAN MUST WRECK YOU!

IT'S A TRICK! SMASH HIM!

YOU FEEL THAT FIGHTING ME WHEN I DO NOT DESIRE TO FIGHT WILL MAKE YOU BRAVE?

BUT...

BAF!

BRAVERY IS THE TRUTH SHE FINDS IN HER OWN HEART.

NOTHUNG!

THE END

THE ICE KING & HIS MAGICAL MATCHMAKING MINI-COMIC

ISSUE TWELVE, COVER C

LILLI CARRÉ

COMICS! Who wants some comics?!

Me!

Me!

OoOoo...

ooo...

oOO...

oOO...

ooo....

Soon, everyone will be so entranced by my comic that I'll be able to steal the princess and NO ONE will notice!!!

WHOOPS! Looks like I've run out.

I'll go get some more!

COMICS

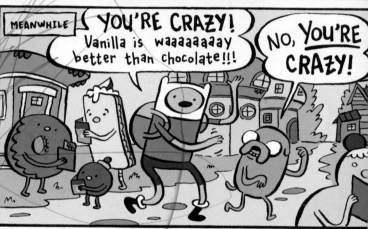

MEANWHILE

YOU'RE CRAZY! Vanilla is waaaaaaaay better than chocolate!!!

NO, YOU'RE CRAZY!

Whatever. You'll eat anything. Vanilla is WAYYY better because you can add all sorts of flavors to it.

Strawberries, cookies, cookie dough...

?

Hey, watch it!

You ran into me!!!

Butterscotch, caramel... You can even add as much chocolate as you—

??!

SHHHH!

WHAT THE HECK?! WHO DID THAT?

Easy, Finn.

NO ONE "**SHUSHES**" ME! I HAVE THINGS TO SAY!

Hmm, what's this?

Important things like... Uh...

Mind if I borrow this? Thanks!

Active rubrix, Super-Pack, flagellum...

SHH!!! I'M TRYING TO READ!

WHAT THE-?! Why do I keep getting shushed?!

What's going on here...?

It seems as though everyone is entranced by these little comic books.

The Ice King is Awesome? Sounds... Interesting...?

:BLINK!: :BLINK!:

GIVE THAT BACK!

HEY!

I was reading that!

But I was reading it first!

POW! BAM! WHAM!

RRRIP!!!

WAIT! Do we know <u>how</u> to make a minicomic?

EASY, JAKE! As a matter of fact, **I DO!**

Now, if you'll allow me...

STEP 1 Figure out how long your comic will be by writing a page-by-page summary of your story.

TIP! To avoid having blank pages, make sure your pages are divisible by four.

MATHE-MATICAL!

STEP 2 Take a stack of paper and fold it in half to make a little book.

FOLD!

STEP 3 Count the pages to see if you have enough for your comic. Add or remove pages as needed.

6   7

Then, number the pages of your book.

STEP 4 Unfold the pages and begin drawing your comic on the correct pages.

aw e 2   Draw page 11   Draw page 4

Draw page 9

2   11   4   9

TIP! Don't worry: the comic will seem out of order. It will make sense as a book!

STEP 5 After you finish drawing your comic, stack the papers with even numbers on the left starting with page 2, until all your paper is stacked.

6   7   4   9   2   11

STEP 6 To make a cover, take a single sheet of paper and fold it in half. Unfold the paper and draw on the right half of the page.

BOO!

STEP 7 Take the stack of comic pages and flip the stack over so page 1 is on top. Place the cover on top.

STEP 8 Make double-sided copies of your stack of pages.

TIP!

Many libraries have copiers that can make double-sided copies. Look for one that has an automatic feed!

STEP 9 Take the copy of your comic and fold it in half.

FOLD!

TIP!

Use a spoon to help flatten out the fold.

STEP 10 Open up your comic and — using a long neck stapler — staple twice along the fold, stapling the pages together.

TIP!

Libraries will usually have these!

STEP 11 Read through your comic and make sure all the pages are in order. Then, continue to make more copies, until **ALL** of your fans are satisfied!!!

I got some paper, pens, and Pencils!

COOL!

I have a ruler and long neck stapler!

I'm going to draw that one time we kicked the Ice King's butt.

Hee hee.

I'm going to draw that one time I ate that pastry that was so good it made me cry.

YUM!

Many days later...

YES!

Z Z Z Z

WE'VE DONE IT!!!

We've created the ULTIMATE minicomic!

Our comic makes the Ice King look like a chump!

Now, it's time to distribute them.

And so, Finn and Jake distributed their comics all throughout the land...

ENJOY!

END

THE DEVILISH DEVOURER
OF DELICIOUS DELICACIES

THE PRINCESS OF
RAD HATS

ISSUE FOURTEEN, COVER D
MING DOYLE

FINN & JAKE
"THE PRINCESS OF RAD HATS"

Whoa, whoa, back up there, Stony Stetson.

What's the matter, Finn? You like hats. Especially rad hats!

I love rad hats! Rad hats are not the issue.

I can't be a princess

I'm a **boy**!

IT IS WRITTEN

Yeah, Finn. Look, you've got a crown!

Whaaugh! How did **that** get there?

IT IS A PRINCESS CROWN

FOR A **PRETTY PRINCESS**

This stinks! My job is **rescuing** princesses, not **being** them!

Excuse me, your highness...

...I've got your itinerary—

Itenawhatwhat? Who are you?

I'm Cloche, your royal assistant.

You get an **assistant?!** Aw, man, I should've taken credit for defeating that guy!

Yeah, you **really** gotta get that crippling giant hat phobia under control.

A-HEM. Look, Princess Finn, there is a very long list of royal responsibilities to which you must attend.

First, you have to approve the mudflap designs for the royal carriage. Then you must present yourself at the monthly princess meeting —

Designs? Myself? Meetings?

NEVER!

Come on, Jake! Let's go challenge the beards of Beardly Canyon.

Aww yeah! Whenever we do that, we end up with sweet beards on our...

Eh, we'd better not. I don't wanna be responsible for you neglecting your princess duties.

WHAT?!

The citizens of the Kingdom of Rad Hats are counting on you, Finn!

Princess Finn.

Princess Finn.

Fine! Whatever! Let's take a look at these royal mudflaps. Is this one of them?

Yes!

APPROVED!

If we're going to make any real headway in our goal to curb Ooo's toot emissions, we're going to have to make a much more concerted effort.

Some of the kingdoms are producing more than their fair share of toots!

I'm looking at **you**, Princess Fiber!

-GASP-

SLAM

Oh my glob, he's all sweaty

Finn! This meeting is for princesses only!

It's okay, Princess Bubblegum! I'm a princess now. The Princess of Rad Hats!

But the Kingdom of Rad Hats hasn't had a princess since the Millineuromancer seized the throne!

Me and Finn defeated him!

Mostly me.

Oh great, now they'll let anybody be a princess

BEST PRINCESS EVER

BUMP

BUMP
BUMP
BUMP

BUMP
BUMP
BUMP
BUMP

Um...

Cloche?

BUMP
BUMP
BUMP

What are you doing?

BUMP

I'm tired of this foolishness!

Your boisterous enthusiasm for things is **hardly** a suitable trait for the "ruler" of a kingdom as classy as **ours!**

So is this like your version of a **hug** or something? Are you encouraging me to better represent your people?

No, I'm **attacking** you! Whomever defeats the Princess of Rad Hats in single combat becomes the **new** Princess!

BUMP

BUMP

OH
OOOOHHH!

BUMP
BUMP
BUMP

I'm no match for her mighty...

...umm...

her mighty...

BUMP

BUMP

Felt!

Yeah! Yeah, her mighty felt!

"Oh!"

"I have been defeated!"

VANISH!

Ha ha HA HA HA HA HA!

All hail Princess CLOCHE!

On your knees, peons!

You didn't learn any-thing!

My belly hurts.

Heh-heh. "Felt."

END

"MY CIDER THE MOUNTAIN"
Written and Illustrated by Aaron Renier

Aaron lives in Chicago with his best friend Beluga. Most days they can be seen running around the park scaring ducks. Aaron has two graphic novels you can read if you want, the first one is called SPIRAL-BOUND, and the second is THE UNSINKABLE WALKER BEAN. Both are a little weird, but they're fun.
aaronrenier.com

"LAUNDROMARCELINE"
Written and Illustrated by Lucy Knisley

Lucy Knisley is a comic artist and author. She is 27 and lives in New York. Her newest book is called RELISH. Learn way more than you ever wanted to about Lucy at www.lucyknisley.com.

"BACON FIELDS"
Written and Illustrated by Michael DeForge

Michael lives in Toronto, Ontario and works as a prop and effects designer on ADVENTURE TIME. He also draws comics on the side! He spends his time alternating between eating pizza, ordering pizza and thinking about ordering pizza, depending on the time of day. He is trying out a moustache.
kingtrash.com

"ULTIMATE PARTY DIP"
Written and Illustrated by Chris "Elio" Eliopoulos

Chris is a cartoonist from Chicago, IL. He loves drawing comics all day long. Check out his recent graphic novels, OKIE DOKIE DONUTS, GABBA BALL!, and MONSTER PARTY.
eliohouse.com

"EMIT ERUTNEVDA"
Written and Illustrated by Paul Pope

Paul Pope is an artist living and working in New York City, USA. His current project, a graphic novel called BATTLING BOY, will be out next year from First Second Books. His nephews, Ben and Alexander, are huge ADVENTURE TIME fans (hi guys!).
pulphope.blogspot.com

"LEVEL 99"
Written and Illustrated by Anthony Clark

Anthony lives in Indianapolis and draws cartoons about a half-bear/half-potato. You can read those and more at www.nedroid.com, if you are brave enough.

"TIME WAITS FOR NO ONE"
Written and Illustrated by Shannon Wheeler

Shannon Wheeler is the Eisner Award–winning creator of TOO MUCH COFFEE MAN. He has contributed to a variety of publications that include The Onion newspaper and The New Yorker magazine. Wheeler currently lives with his cats, chickens, bees, girlfriend and children. His weekly comic strip is published in various alternative weeklies and online at tmcm.com.

"HAPPY BIRTHDAY HOT DOG PRINCESS!"
Written and Illustrated by Frank Gibson & Becky Dreistadt

Becky and Frank have been together for 7 years and have been making comics for almost as long! They love cartoons, cats, travel and old things. They make a hand-painted webcomic called TINY KITTEN TEETH and recently finished "Capture Creatures," a year-long 151 painting project.
tinykittenteeth.com

"FISHLING"
Written by Shane Houghton
Illustrated by Chris Houghton

Brothers Shane and Chris Houghton are the dynamic duo behind the Image comic book series REED GUNTHER. They have also worked on comics for THE SIMPSONS, PEANUTS, and more!
reedgunther.com

"HOT DEALS IN ICE KINGDOM"
Written by Jon M. Gibson
Illustrated by Jim Rugg

Jim Rugg is the co-creator of AFRODISIAC, THE PLAIN JANES, STREET ANGEL, and USAPE. He is also the co-host of TELL ME SOMETHING I DON'T KNOW. Jon M. Gibson is a writer/director who has done a bunch of seemingly random things with his life: scripts for animated cartoons, lots of articles for the few surviving print magazines, and founded a company called iam8bit, where he makes lots of fun stuff with his great pal, Amanda.
facebook.com/jonmgibson   jimrugg.com

"THE MEANING OF BRAVERY"
Written and Illustrated by Zack Giallongo

Zack Giallongo is a typical bearded cartoonist who plays the banjo and loves animals, both on and off the table. He just released his first graphic novel, BROXO, about teenage barbarians and zombies which somehow made it onto the New York Times Bestseller list.
zackgiallongo.com

"THE ICE KING & HIS MAGICAL MATCHMAKING MINI-COMIC"
Written by Alexis Frederick-Frost
Illustrated by Andrew Arnold

Andrew Arnold and Alexis Frederick-Frost are two heads of the 3-headed cartooning monster responsible for creating the ADVENTURES IN CARTOONING graphic novels from First Second Books. Alexis' other works include writing and drawing a series about the exploits of a worldly wise cat and ever-eager dog in Oxford, UK and creating numerous self-published mini-comics. Andrew's work has appeared in several publications from Roaring Brook Press, Cambridge University Press, and Nickelodeon Magazine, to name a few. He currently lives in New York City and works in publishing.
cartoonstudies.org/arnold/comics.html   cartoonstudies.org/frederickfrost/

"PRINCESS OF RAD HATS"
Written and Illustrated by Chris Schweizer

Chris Schweizer is the author of THE CROGAN ADVENTURES, a historical adventure graphic novel series full of pirates, ninjas, cowboys, and all the things that you probably never got to spend any time on in history class. He also does other stuff, like teach college, and be a dad.
croganadventures.blogspot.com

"AFTER THE SHOW," "THE RIDE OF SIR SLICER," & "LUMPY SPACE DRAMA"
Written and Illustrated by Zac Gorman

Zac Gorman writes the webcomic MAGICAL GAME TIME, designs poster art, and has recently been dipping his toe into character design and other such jobs involving video games, comics and cartoons that are, "seriously, so freakin' awesome to be getting paid to do." His words, not mine. He lives in Chicago.
zacgorman.com

"ICE KINGDUMB"
Written by Georgia & Chris Roberson

Chris Roberson can type very fast (he writes comics like EDISON REX and THE MYSTERIOUS STRANGERS), but Georgia Roberson never lets him forget that she can draw better than he can. When Georgia isn't busy making up stories and drawing, she attends Buckman Arts Focus Elementary in Portland, Oregon.

"THE DEVILISH DEVOURER OF DELICIOUS DELICACIES"
Written and Illustrated by Josh Lesnick

Josh is an artist from Minneapolis who has drawn comics on the internet since 1951. He has much sympathy for the Ice King, because he is also quite fond of princesses, and his friends are all worried about him.

SUGARY SHORTS

Volume Two
COMING IN 2014!